Awesome Animal Stories

KINGFISHER
An imprint of Kingfisher Publications Plc
New Penderel House, 283-288 High Holborn
London WC1V 7HZ
www.kingfisherpub.com

First published by Kingfisher 2007
2 4 6 8 10 9 7 5 3 1

A CIP catalogue record for this book is available from
the British Library.

ISBN: 978 0 7534 1508 5

Printed in China
1TR/0707/PROSP/MAR/80NEWSP/C

SUPER SHORTS

Awesome Animal Stories

compiled by Elizabeth Holland
Illustrated by Kate Pankhurst

KINGFISHER

Contents

Crocodile Tears

Joyce Dunbar

Two mother crocodiles were basking
by the river, their jaws wide open
in the sun.

They were very proud crocodiles,
because their eggs had successfully
hatched, and in each of their mouths
was a tiny baby crocodile.

But these mother crocodiles had a
problem. It was time for their babies
to leave the comfortable pouch in

their jaws and join the other baby crocodiles in the swamp, but the babies just wouldn't let go. They were frightened of the big wide world.

The mother crocodiles looked at each other, chewing over their problem. This in itself wasn't easy, for it is very hard to chew anything at all when you have a lot of sharp teeth and a small baby crocodile in your mouth.

Crocodile Tears

"I've never known a baby so clinging," said the first mother crocodile. "He wants me to carry him everywhere."

"Mine's just the same," said the second mother crocodile. "I've coaxed and cajoled but this baby will not be put down. I have to eat on one side of my mouth. Just try that when you're trying to tuck into a warthog."

"I know how it is," said the first mother crocodile. "So tiresome."

Then, with their jaws still wide open in the sun, cosily cradling their babies, the mother crocodiles went to sleep.

A crocodile bird came along, pick-pick-picking at the teeth of the first mother crocodile for bits of food left between the teeth. Her baby didn't like this. They were his bits of food. He gave a snap with his baby jaws, but the crocodile bird escaped.

It flew to the
second mother
crocodile's jaws.
Pick-pick-pick it
went again.

The second mother's baby also
gave a sharp snap with his baby jaws.
Again the crocodile bird escaped.

"Yah! Missed!" said the first baby
crocodile to the second baby
crocodile.

"So did you!" said the second
baby crocodile, peeping between his
mother's teeth.

"What if I did?" said the first
baby crocodile. "My mum's bigger
than yours."

"What if she is bigger?" said the second baby crocodile. "My mum's scalier than yours."

"What if she is scalier?" said the first baby crocodile. "My mum can swim faster than yours. She catches more fish."

"Well, my mum caught a shark this morning," said the second baby crocodile. "And she ate it all, and that was just for breakfast."

"I don't believe you," said the first baby crocodile. "There aren't any sharks around here. Anyway, my mum frightened some people this morning. Three people in a boat. She frightened them away."

"Did she only frighten them?" said the first baby crocodile. My mum catches people. She catches them and puts them in the larder."

"No, she doesn't," said the second baby crocodile. "Because my mum went looking in your mum's larder yesterday and there weren't any people there. There was only a skinny water rat."

"Oh, did your mum go looking in my mum's larder?"

said the first baby crocodile. "Well, I'll tell my mum when she wakes up. My mum will take a bite out of your mum."

"Oh, will she?" said the second baby crocodile. "I'd like to see her try. My mum's got a lot more teeth than your mum."

"How do you know that?" said the first crocodile. "You can't count!"

"Oh, yes I can!" said the second baby crocodile. "Three. A hundred.

Seventy-one. Four thousand."

"Well, my mum's teeth are sharper and longer than your mum's teeth, so there!"

"How do you know that?" said the second baby crocodile. "You can't measure!"

"Just you come along here and take a look!" said the first baby crocodile.

"I will an' all," said the second baby crocodile, "and you just come along here and take a look."

"I will an' all," said the first baby crocodile. By this time, the two baby crocodiles had forgotten all about how frightened they were of the big wide world. The first baby crocodile slithered out of his mother's jaws and started to make his way to the jaws of the second mother crocodile.

The second baby crocodile slithered out of his mother's jaws and started to make his way to the jaws of the first mother crocodile.

They passed each other on the way.

"Hey, look!" said the first baby crocodile. "We're down on the ground!"

"So we are!" said the second baby crocodile. "On our own four legs!"

They swished their tails and snapped their jaws happily at each other.

"There's the swamp," said the first baby crocodile, "and a whole lot more baby crocodiles. Why don't we go for a splash?"

"We can count teeth later," said the second baby crocodile, belly-crawling along after him.

The crocodile bird saw his chance. Pick-pick-pick he went on the first mother's teeth, then pick-pick-pick on the other.

Suddenly, the mothers woke up.

Crocodile Tears

"Where's my baby?" said the first mother crocodile.

"Where's mine?" said the second mother crocodile.

They raced down to the edge of the swamp. There they found the two baby crocodiles, playing and splashing with all the other baby crocodiles.

"Ah! Aren't they sweet?" they said to each other, grinning from eye to eye.

Then they wept great crocodile tears.

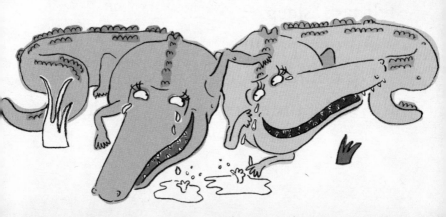

The Lamb Who Couldn't Sleep

John Yeoman

It was springtime on the marshes, and every day the young lambs raced around the fields and jumped and turned in the air. Every evening, they settled down beside their mothers, out of the wind, and fell fast asleep.

All except one.

He could never get to sleep at the right time. Instead, he would lie

awake listening to the snores coming
from all the other sheep in the field.
No matter how hard he tried, he
just didn't seem to be able to fall
asleep. What was worse, just as the
first faint light of the sun began to
appear over the hedge and the mist
began to clear from the field, he
would start to doze off.

Every morning
began the same
way.

"Time to get up," said his mother. "It's going to be a lovely morning. Have a little drink and nibble some fresh grass and then you can go off and play with your friends."

Through his sleepy, half-opened eyes, the lamb could see some of his friends already at their leaping and spinning around the field.

"I don't think I want to play yet," he said, and gave a big yawn.

"Oh dear," said his mother. "Didn't you sleep very well?"

"No," he said. "I didn't sleep at all. I never do."

"Why don't you try counting sheep tonight?" his mother suggested.

That night he took his mother's advice. As he snuggled down beside her, sheltered from the breeze, he began to count. Because he was a very young lamb he could only count up to three, but he thought that counting up to three over and over again was probably as good as counting up to a hundred once.

"One, two, THREE . . . one, two, THREE . . . one, two, THREE . . . one, two, THREE."

"What does that young idiot think he's doing?" came the voice of a sheep out of the darkness.

"Sounds like he's starting a race," came a reply.

"Is he trying to get us to join in a song?" suggested another.

"I think you're keeping the others awake," his mother whispered. "That's enough counting for tonight."

The lamb just sighed, rested his chin on his front feet, and settled down to another sleepless night.

After breakfast the next morning he staggered across the field to say hello to his friends. But his eyes were so bleary and his legs were so unsteady that he stumbled right into a big oak tree.

"It isn't good manners to go bumping into people's homes like that," said a voice from above.

The lamb looked up and saw an owl sitting on a branch.

"I'm very sorry," said the lamb. "I'm so tired that I didn't see the tree."

"How can you be tired?" snapped the owl. "You haven't done anything yet!"

25

"I didn't sleep. I never do."

"Deary me," said the owl in a softer voice. "We shall have to do something about that. Come back to see me this afternoon, and I'll give you some of my special sleeping mixture."

"Oh, thank you," said the lamb.

And he set off to join his friends, feeling much better already.

Back at the oak tree after lunch, he was a little disappointed to find that the owl hadn't been able to make his special sleeping mixture.

"It's nearly ready," the bird explained, "but I'm afraid I'm short of one or two items. Would you be

good enough to bring me a feather
which has dropped from a crow,
please? That fellow there has a loose
one sticking out, do you see?"

The lamb raced after the
crow, which waited
until he was near
before flying up
and landing a
few feet
away.

The lamb gave chase again and the crow did exactly the same thing. It happened again and again, until finally the feather came free and fluttered to the ground.

Quick as a flash the lamb picked it up in his mouth and ran back to the tree.

"Well done," said the owl. "Just leave it there while you go for the other thing."

"You mean there's more?" panted the lamb.

"Well, you want the mixture to work properly, don't you?" asked the owl. Yes, the lamb certainly wanted the mixture to work properly.

"Good," said the owl. "Now, you see that black lamb over there? He's got a particular kind of thistle sticking to his fleece. Just bring me that, and then we're ready."

The lamb bounded off again. When the black lamb saw him coming, he thought it was a game and raced away as fast as he could. They ran and ran, this way and that across the field, for ages and ages –

until finally the thistle dropped off and the lamb was able to pick it up.

He returned to the tree, all hot and puffed out.

"That's exactly what we need," said the owl. "Unfortunately, it's too late this afternoon to finish making the mixture. But you shall have it tomorrow. Go back to your mother now."

It was getting dark when the lamb got back to his mother.

"Had a nice afternoon?" she asked.

And do you know, he was so worn out that he just lay down and fell asleep.

★ ★ ★

The Lamb Who Couldn't Sleep

The next morning he was completely refreshed from his good night's sleep and couldn't wait to tell the owl.

"I slept soundly all night!" he said.

"I thought you might," said the owl, with a wink. "So you won't be needing my mixture after all. You see, it's my belief that you'll sleep well every night from now on."

And the wise old owl was right. The lamb spent every day chasing around with his friends, and every night he fell asleep as soon as he closed his eyes.

And I hope you do too.

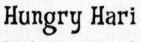

Hungry Hari

Dick King-Smith

Hari was just about the largest python in the Indian jungle. From his broad snout to the tip of his tail, Hari was ten metres long.

Not only was he an enormous snake, he also had an enormous appetite. Like all pythons, he would lie in wait to catch his prey, and squeeze

it to death,
and then swallow it whole.

Goats, pigs, deer – it didn't
matter how big they were.
Hari would unlock his jaws
and in would go the poor
animal head first, to end up as
a goat-shaped or pig-shaped or
deer-shaped lump in the
middle of that ten-metre-long
body.

Sometimes Hari climbed into
the trees, for a little snack of birds'
eggs, and birds too if he could catch
them, but especially monkeys. Hari
hated monkeys.

They hung around,
shouting rude things at him
and telling the other animals
of the jungle where he was.

"Watch out, the giant worm is
coming!" they cried, and they
followed Hari about, calling him
"Nolegs!" and throwing nuts and
fruit and twigs at him.

There was one particular monkey
that hungry Hari hated more than
any other. Her name was Veneeta,

and she was young and
very quick and very,
very bold. She alone of
all the monkeys dared
not just to tease, but to
touch the enormous python.

It happened one sultry afternoon
when the jungle creatures were
sheltering from the burning sun,
and dozing in the shade of the giant
trees. Hari had just caught and killed
a young nilghai, a kind of large forest
antelope, and was settling down to
eat it.

Veneeta sat with all her friends on a branch overhead, and they watched as Hari gradually got himself around his huge meal.

"Hope it sticks in his throat," said one of the monkeys.

"He'd be really choked!" said another, and they all chattered with laughter.

"Nolegs!" they shouted at Hari, and "Nobrains!" and they danced about on the branch and made faces.

All the time the nilghai moved slowly along inside Hari until at last it stopped, a nilghai-shaped lump right in the middle of his

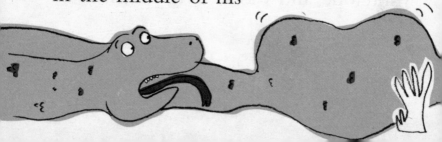

ten-metre-long body.

"Now," said Veneeta, "watch me, you lot."

"What are you going to do?" asked the others.

"Pull his tail," said Veneeta.

"You wouldn't dare!" they said.

"Wait and see," she said, and she ran down the tree, quick as a flash, grabbed hold of the tip of Hari's tail and gave it a tweak.

The news spread round the jungle like wildfire. Veneeta the monkey had dared to tweak hungry Hari's tail!

The peacocks, whose call is very loud, flew up into the treetops and cried the tidings, so that everyone knew, from the smallest forest-shrew

to the mighty tiger.

And now, wherever Hari went, all the creatures of the jungle would mock him, telling him he needed eyes in the back of his head.

"Look out for Veneeta!" they cried. "She can't pull your leg, but she'll pull your tail again if you don't watch out!"

And she did. Each time she would wait until Hari had had a long meal and there was a something-shaped lump in the middle of that long, long body. And then, knowing how sluggish he would be with a full belly, Veneeta would nip down and grab the tip of his tail.

At first she only pulled it, but one day, growing yet more daring, she actually gave it a nip, sinking her sharp little teeth in the extreme end of hungry Hari before darting away while all her friends cheered and jeered.

Once again the peacocks cried the amazing news. Veneeta the monkey had dared to bite hungry Hari's tail! What next? Would she dance upon his body perhaps, this cheeky Veneeta? Would she run

along its ten-metre-length and bite
him on the nose and be gone before
the giant worm could catch her?

To catch Veneeta became the most
important thing in Hari's life. Every
night now he slithered among the
branches of the great trees, looking
for her. Many a monkey went
headlong down that endless throat,
but never the one he wanted, the
one he hated, the one that had had
the impudence to bite the tip of
his tail.

Then there came a morning when hungry Hari lay asleep on the forest floor. In the trees above, cheeky Veneeta and the other monkeys hid and watched. The python was lying in thick undergrowth, so that Veneeta could see only his great

blunt head at one end and his tail-tip at the other. What shape of lump there might be in the middle, she could not see.

In fact there was no lump, for

Hari had had a poor night's hunting,
catching only a single monkey
whose body was too small to alter
his shape.

Should I risk it? Veneeta thought.
That tail-tip was so tempting. She
jumped down, but as she jumped,

Hari stirred. Some instinct told him
that his hated tormentor was near.

He looked about, half asleep still,
and he stretched, flexing the million
muscles in his long, long body, from

his head to the end of his tail, which twitched.

Veneeta saw the movement of the tail-tip, and so did Hari. With lightning speed, he struck.

"Look!" cried Veneeta to all her friends. "The python is eating himself!"

So hungry was Hari that at first he did not realize what he was doing. So wide open were his jaws that he could not see what it was he was swallowing.

That monkey's taking a long time to go down, he said to himself, *and what's more, my tail feels as though something's eating it.*

Then suddenly he saw Veneeta dancing around him, while up above her friends cheered and jeered. Only then, when two or three of his ten metres were inside him, did hungry

Hari understand what was happening.

By now the peacocks had spread the news throughout the jungle, and all the creatures, from the smallest forest-shrew to the mighty tiger, came to watch the amazing sight of hungry Hari the python devouring himself.

Everyone watched intently, except Veneeta, who was now so excited that she did not notice that Hari had stopped swallowing his tail and was beginning to pull it back out again.

"Look at old Nolegs!" she cried to them all, turning her back on the python. "Look at old Nobrains! You know the trouble with him, don't you? He's too full of himself!"

Then suddenly everyone saw the danger that the cheeky monkey was in, and called out to warn her.

"Veneeta, Veneeta!" they all cried, which sounded to Hari, who was rather deaf, like "Eat her! Eat her!"

In the nick of time Veneeta leapt into the air as the python's great blunt head whizzed underneath her.

"Misssssed," said hungry Hari softly, as Veneeta and her friends swung away through the trees. "But I'll sssssswallow you one day, sssssee if I don't."

He never did, though.

For while cheeky Veneeta still

shouted rude things at hungry Hari
whenever she saw him, there was one
thing she never dared to touch again.

You know what it was, don't you?

The end of that tail.

(And that's the end of this tale.)

Hot Hippos

Sally Grindley

It was hot. Very, very hot. The lions were hot, the giraffes were hot, the zebras were hot. But hottest of all were the hippos. And a hot hippo is not a happy hippo.

"When is it going to rain?" grumbled Harriet. "All this sun is making my skin feel like an elephant's bottom."

"I don't think it's ever going to

rain again," moaned Henry. "Soon the last drop of water in the lake will have dried up, and then where will we be?"

The lake was now so small that only one hippo could fit in it at a time. The hippos had drawn up a rota and were taking it in turns to go for a wallow. Hepzibah was the lucky hippo wallowing now while the others sweltered.

"Soon be my turn," said Harriet.

"Five more minutes, Hepzi."

"Well, don't splash this time," said Hepzibah. "You wasted a lot of water bouncing around last time."

"I'm not waiting for my next turn," said Henry. "I'm off. I don't want to look like a shrivelled prune."

Hepzibah and Harriet looked at him in astonishment.

"You're going?" said Harriet. "But where? We've always lived here. How will you find another lake? You might get lost."

"Better than staying here," said Henry. "That puddle will be gone by tomorrow, and there's hardly any grass left to eat."

Harriet frowned and shed a hot salty tear that instantly dried on her hot hippo skin. She looked at Hepzibah. Even though she had bunched herself up to make herself as small as possible, there was no room in the water for her bottom.

Only her feet and ample tummy were submerged. She had to accept that their once magnificent lake was now no more than a pitiful puddle.

But it was still all the water they had and she was terrified at the thought of leaving it.

Then Hepzibah heaved her hefty bulk out of the water and said, "You're right, Henry. No point in staying here to wallow in self-pity – and that's all there will be to wallow in. I'm coming too."

"What about you, Harriet?" said Henry. "You can't stay here on your own. As soon as the sun goes down and it's cooler, we'll set off."

Late that evening, the three hippos each

took one final lingering roll in the shrinking puddle, tore at the last few threads of brown grass, and began their long, slow journey in search of water and food. They walked at night, munched on any bits of greenery they could find in the evening and early morning, and sat under trees and dozed when the midday sun made it too hot to do anything.

Four days passed and the hippos were growing weaker and weaker. They ached all over from so much walking, their bellies rumbled with hunger, their feet were sore and blistered, and their dry, cracked skin hung loosely from them as they grew thinner and thinner. They began to give up hope that they would ever find water again, when one evening Henry suddenly stopped and pointed.

"Look, what's that? Over there. Behind those trees. There's something shiny. Stay there while I go and see."

He bounded through the undergrowth as fast as a tired, hot and hungry hippo could go, and when he reached the other side of the trees he

stopped
and shouted
back, "It's water!
Come and see, it's water!"

And with that he leapt into the
water and rolled and splashed and
kicked and gurgled and behaved just
like a small child in a swimming
pool. Hepzibah and Harriet weren't
far behind, and when they reached
the water they jumped in with loud
squeals of delight. Just at that moment
it would have been difficult to find
three happier hippos anywhere.

That night they went to sleep
under the trees, and in the early
morning they explored their new
home. The lake wasn't as big as
their old one, but there were two
more next to it, and all around there
was lush green grass and beautiful
trees and bushes. When the day
began to warm up, they sat in the
lake and thought how good life was.
Then they spotted something they

had never seen before. It was like rain, but it was all coming from one spot and it was going up into the air and round and round.

Hepzibah couldn't contain herself. She leapt from the lake, bounded across the grass and danced around under the spray in a strange sort of hippo rumba.

That's when it happened. Something hard hit Harriet on her snout.

"Ouch," she cried. "That hurt. Who's throwing things?"

Then the same thing happened to Henry. "Oy," he cried. "Someone's throwing things." And he picked what looked like a round, white stone out of the water.

The two hippos looked around them, and suddenly saw two people walking towards the lake carrying metal sticks in their hands and long bags over their backs.

"This looks like trouble," said Henry. "Duck."

Harriet and Henry both ducked quickly, but Hepzibah was blissfully unaware that she was about to be spotted.

"Hey, what's that under the sprinkler?" a first voice cried.

"Well, bless my soul," exclaimed the other voice. "That looks like a hippo to me. And look, there's another one, and another one. How on earth did they get there?"

The two men ran off to tell the world, leaving the hippos to wonder what would happen.

Before very long, crowds of people lined the golf course, trying to catch a glimpse of the hippos. Great cheers went up every time Henry, Harriet and Hepzibah raised their heads from the lake. Some of the golfers grew angry because so many people were wandering over the greens that they couldn't get on with their game, and they had to miss out three of the holes because they were scared to go too close to the hippos.

The golfers wanted to have the hippos taken away, but everyone else was so angry at the suggestion that the golfers were forced to leave them where they were. A special enclosure was put up around the hippos' lake to protect them, and the golfers just had to put up with a slight alteration to their course and one lake fewer.

As for the hippos, they had water and they had grass and they soon learned that if a golfer shouted the warning FORE, they should duck right under the water to avoid a painful blow on the head.

The Magpie's Nest

Michael Rosen

Once, a long time ago, when winter was nearly over and spring had nearly begun, all the birds were busy starting to build their nests. There they all were: the robin and the eagle, the seagull, the blackbird, the duck, the owl and the hummingbird, all busy. All that is, except Magpie. And she didn't feel much like working.

It was a nice day and she was out and about looking for scrips and scraps and bibs and bobs for her collection of old junk – her hoard of bits and pieces she had picked up from behind chimneys or from drainpipes. Pebbles, beads, buttons and the like, anything bright and interesting or unusual, Magpie was sure to collect. Just as she was flying along on the lookout for a new treasure, she caught sight of Sparrow, her mouth full of bits of straw and twigs.

"What are you doing, what are you doing?" said Magpie.

"Building my nest," said Sparrow,

"like you'll have to soon."

"Oh yes?" said Magpie.

"Yes," said Sparrow, "put that
milk-bottle-top down and come
over here and watch. First you have
to find a twig, and then another
twig, another twig, another twig,
another twig . . ."

"Don't make me laugh," said
Magpie, "I know, I know, I know all
that," and off she flew. And as she
flew on looking for scrips and
scraps and bibs and bobs she came

up to Duck, who was upside down with her mouth full of mud.

"What are you doing, what are you doing?" said Magpie.

"Building my nest," said Duck, "like you'll have to do soon."

"Oh yes?" said Magpie.

"Yes," said Duck, "throw away that old earwig and watch me. After you've got all your twigs you have to stick them with mud pats like this – pat-pat, pat-pat, pat-pat . . ."

"Don't make me laugh," said Magpie, "I know, I know, I know all that," and off she flew. And as she flew on looking for scrips and scraps and bibs and bobs she saw Pigeon with a mouthful of feathers.

"What are you doing, what are you doing?" said Magpie.

"Building my nest," said Pigeon, "like you'll have to soon."

"Oh yes?" said Magpie.

"Yes," said Pigeon, "put that bus ticket down and come over here and learn how. You have to make yourself warm and cosy – right? Right. So you dig your beak into your chest like this – right? And find one of those very soft fluffy feathers down there and you lay those out very carefully inside your nest to keep it warm and cosy, warm and cosy, warm and cosy . . ."

"Don't make me laugh," said Magpie. "I know, I know, I know all that," and off she flew.

Well, not long after that it was time for Magpie to lay her eggs and she looked out from her perch and saw all the other birds sitting in their well-built, warm, cosy nests, laying their eggs. "Oh no," said Magpie, "I haven't got anywhere to lay mine! I'd better hurry." And she remembered Sparrow saying something about

twigs, and Duck about patting them and Pigeon saying something about cosy feathers. So she rushed out and quickly grabbed as many twigs as she could, made a great pile of them, threw a feather on the top – and the milk-bottle-top and the earwig and the bus ticket, and she just had time to sit herself down and lay her eggs.

And if you look at a magpie's nest, you'll see it's always a mess. And she ends up throwing her scrips and scraps and bibs and bobs in it too.

I think she likes it like that.

Slowly Does It

Robin Ravilious

Something had invaded the forest; something strange and worrying. The Howler Monkey heard it. The Jaguar smelled it. The Macaws saw something moving in the bushes. But no one could tell what it was.

The Something had a strange smell; it left strange tracks; and it made noises that the forest had never heard before. The animals didn't like it at all.

At last the Jaguar – who was bigger and stronger than the rest – called a meeting to decide what to do. Everyone gathered round nervously. Everyone except the Sloth, that is. He was asleep, as usual, in his tree.

"Well!" growled the Jaguar in his deep fierce voice. "Does anyone know what this Something is?"

"It's much taller than a monkey," said the Howler Monkey.

"It has a shiny yellow head," said a Macaw.

"It makes a terrible snarling noise," said a Marmoset. "But sometimes it whistles like a bird."

"It smells bad, like fire," said a Snake.

Then the Jaguar asked the question they were most worried about. "What does it eat?"

The animals looked at each other in silence. No one knew what it ate. They just hoped it ate nothing but fruit. The fact was that no one had seen it properly at all.

Then the Jaguar had an idea.
"What about that good-for-
nothing Sloth?" he growled. "He's
been hanging about for weeks.
He must have seen it. Go and call
the Sloth."

Everyone looked up, and there,
high above them in the tallest tree,
was a dirty-looking bundle of hair
hanging from a branch. The Howler
Monkey went tearing up.

"Hey, you! Slowcoach!" he yelled,
shaking the Sloth's branch. "Shift
your bulk. Jaguar wants a word
with you."

The Sloth was hanging peacefully

by his long
shaggy arms
and legs, with
his head resting
on his shaggy
chest. Sometimes he ate the leaves
he could reach. Mostly he just hung
there, fast asleep. He had hung so
still for so long that green mould
was growing in his hair. He took no
notice whatsoever of the Howler
Monkey.

The Howler Monkey shouted and
bounced till fruit rained down on
the animals below, but the Sloth
slept on.

Then all the little
Marmosets went
scampering up to try
waking him. "Quick,
quick, quick!" they
chattered, jumping from
twig to twig like
grasshoppers.

The Sloth opened his
short-sighted eyes. Then
he shut them again.

The Tree Snake went
next, coiling and
twisting up the tree, and
out along the branch.

"I sshould sstop this
ssnoozing," he

whispered in the Sloth's ear. "Better ssafe than ssorry."

The Sloth just opened his mouth in a long, slow-motion yawn.

Then the Macaws had a go. They flew round and round the Sloth, flashing their bright wings and squawking fit to choke.

"Wake up, Slug-a-bed, WAKE UP! Jaguar wants to talk."

The Sloth unhooked one arm and scratched his tummy drowsily.

Then the Jaguar lost his temper. He leapt and clawed his way up the tree, lashing his tail with rage.

"Look here, you mouldy old hammock," he roared. "Are you

going to talk, or do I have to make you?"

The Sloth peered at his visitor. "Good . . . morning," he said slowly (although it was afternoon by now). "What . . . seems . . . to . . . be . . . the . . . trouble?"

All the animals burst out talking at once: growling, yelling, hissing, chattering and squawking about the Something. The Sloth just hung there smiling, and slowly blinking his eyes.

The rumpus went on for some time, for the Sloth wasn't very bright. It took a while to get a new idea into his shaggy head.

"A . . . Something?" he said at last. "What . . . sort . . . of . . ."

"Stop!" interrupted the Howler Monkey. "Listen!"

Everyone went quiet. Up from the ground far beneath them came a noise more terrifying than anything they had ever heard before. An ugly, ear-splitting, snarling roar it was, and it filled them with fear. Then

there was a loud crack, a huge
crash, and one of the nearby trees
just . . . fell down. The animals
could not believe
their eyes.

"The Something,"
whispered the
Jaguar, with his
fur standing on
end. "It's
eating the
trees."

At that,
they all fled in
panic, tumbling helter-skelter
through the branches to get away.
In a moment they were all gone.

All except the Sloth, of course. He was left hanging there alone, with his mouth open, and his question unanswered.

"Nobody . . . tells . . . me . . . anything," he sighed. "I . . . s'pose . . . I'd . . . better . . . go . . . and . . . see . . . "

Then, at last, he started to move. Inch by inch he crept along his branch until he reached the main trunk. The awful noise went on and on, but he took no notice. He wrapped his shaggy arms around the tree and began to climb down. Slowly – oh so slowly – he groped his way down, and down . . . and down.

It was dark under the trees, and the noise had stopped, but still he toiled on. He was nearly there, and feeling so tired, when into the clearing came . . . the Something. They stared at each other.

What the Sloth saw was a man. A man with a chainsaw for cutting down trees. But the Sloth didn't know it was a man. He'd never met one before. He peered at it doubtfully. Then he did what sloths always do to stay out of trouble: he kept quite still and smiled.

But what the man saw, however, in the shadowy forest, far from home, was a horrible hairy hobgoblin

leering at him with a spooky grin on its face. It made his blood run cold. He let out a strangled cry, and ran for his life.

Next morning the other animals came anxiously creeping back. They sniffed the air for that frightening smell. They listened for the frightening noise. But all they smelled were sweet forest scents; and all they heard were the friendly forest calls. The Something had gone. And there was the Sloth, dangling from his branch in the sunshine, slowly stuffing leaves into his smile.

The Little Elephant's Next Best Thing

Mary Rayner

There was once a little elephant who lived in the hills of South India with his mother and all his aunties, in the teak forest.

One day, he was splashing about in the river while his mother was being bathed. He squirted water at the other young elephants, and they squealed and squirted back. Then the little elephant looked up

and saw a
balloon
floating high in
the sky. And
underneath the balloon
was a basket, and in the basket,
just looking at the view, was a
man. *I should like to do that*,
thought the little elephant.
*It would be better than splashing,
better than squirting. It would be the
next best thing to flying.*
He asked his mother how he

could go up in a balloon.

"Don't be silly," said his mother. "You are too small."

So the little elephant waited for the weeks to go by, and then he asked one of his aunties.

"Don't be silly," said the aunty. "You are too heavy."

Oh dear, thought the little elephant. *First I was too small and now I'm too heavy. I shall eat less, and then I will be able to go up in the balloon.*

So he stopped crunching up bamboo leaves, and every time he was hungry he thought about floating through the sky, until the man who looked after the elephants said, "Dear me, this little elephant is getting too thin. Little elephant, what is the matter?"

The little elephant said, "I want to be thin because then I will not be too heavy to go up in a balloon."

"Ay yai," said the man. "But little elephant, you are growing up, you will soon be too big."

The little elephant began to cry.

"It is not too late," said the man kindly. "We will get a balloon made. Soon, soon. All we need is money." So he thought and he thought, and then he said, "Little elephant, come with me, and we shall go to the town."

They waved goodbye to the little elephant's mother and all the aunties, and set off together for the big town. They walked along the hot dusty road for miles and miles, past fields of sugar cane and groves of coconut palms and across a dry river bed.

"I am thirsty," said the little elephant.

"Soon, soon, we shall be there," said the man.

They came to a stall beside the road, next to a garage. The elephant man asked for a cup of tea, and a drink for his elephant. The elephant filled his trunk with water from a bucket, squirted the water into his mouth and drank it all down. The man fetched some more.

Just then a bus drew up, full of people. The driver got out and said, "I need more petrol, and no one can see out of the windows because they are so dusty."

The little elephant became very excited. "I will squirt the windows clean," he said to his friend.

"Tell all your passengers to give money," said the elephant man, "and my elephant will clean your bus."

So the little elephant squirted water all over the bus, and all the passengers were pleased, and gave baksheesh to the elephant man.

When the bus had gone the garage man said, "That was good. If you would like to stay in the compound behind my stall and garage, you can clean all the buses which stop here. Everyone likes your elephant."

So the elephant man and the little elephant stayed for many weeks, until they had cleaned a great many buses and saved up a great deal of money.

"Now it is time to go to the

town," said the elephant man. They waved goodbye to the garage man and set off again along the hot dusty road to the town. They went to find the man who made hot air balloons.

The elephant man explained that the little elephant wanted to ride in a balloon.

The balloon-maker shook his head. "That is not possible," he said. "Your elephant is too heavy."

"Can you not make me one specially?" asked the elephant man.

"Not possible," said the balloon-maker.

"We can pay," said the elephant man, and he tipped out fat bundles of rupees in a heap on the ground.

"Perhaps possible after all," said the balloon-maker. "Come back in three weeks."

The little elephant and his friend went away, and they waited for three weeks, and then they came back again.

The balloon-maker had made a beautiful orange-and-yellow balloon. It lay on the ground

behind the shop and tied onto it
was an enormous basket, an
elephant-sized basket with some
extra space for the elephant man.

"Now I will tell you how to do
it," said the balloon-maker, and he
showed them how to fill the
balloon with hot air to make it
rise up into the sky.

So the balloon was filled with hot air, and just as it lifted off the ground the little elephant and his friend scrambled into the basket. Up into the sky they went, and they waved goodbye to the balloon-maker. Slowly all the white houses of the town and even the big palace became tiny, tinier than toys. They floated along above the dusty road, over the dry river bed and over the coconut palms and over the sugar-cane fields until they came towards the hills.

On their way they saw the garage and the stall, and they

waved, and the garage man waved back and cheered and clapped. And they passed a bus full of tourists, and they waved, and the bus driver and all the tourists waved back and cheered and clapped.

It was just getting to be evening when at last they came to the teak forest. Now they could see the river. They came down a little lower, and the little elephant began to squeal and trumpet, because he could see his mother and all the aunties being bathed.

All the big old elephants looked up, and they saw the great orange-

and-yellow balloon, and the little
elephant waving his trunk, and his
friend beside him.

"Just look at my son!" said
his mother, and she put up her
trunk and trumpeted to him.

The balloon came down on the ground, and the little elephant climbed out. His mother and all the aunties welcomed him back, and all the young elephants had an extra splashy and squirty game with him because he had been away for so long.

The Hedgehog's Race

Duncan Williamson

If you were to travel the hills of
Scotland today you would find
that hedgehogs and hares live
together. They're great friends.
It wasn't always so . . .

Early every morning, old Mr
Brown Hare came down from his
bed in the hillside. He was bound
for the farmer's field because his

breakfast was turnips. He loved the
young turnips coming up, the
leaves. But this one morning, bright
and early, as old Mr Hare came
hopping down the hillside, a
beautiful sunny morning, the
first person he met was old
Mr Hedgehog. And he was
crawling around the

hedgerows hunting for his
breakfast – snails and slugs and
worms, which hedgehogs love to
eat! Because Mr Hare was feeling
very frisky this morning, he
rubbed his paws together and said
to himself, *Oh ho, old Mr Hedgehog!
I'm going to have some fun to myself
this morning!* He liked to tease old
Mr Hedgehog, you know!

So when he came down to the
gate leading to the farmer's field
old Mr Hedgehog of course sat
up with his wee pointed nose
and his little short legs. And old
Mr Hare said, "Good morning,
Short Legs!"

Now hedgehogs are very sensitive about their short legs. And they don't like it very much when somebody talks about them, because their legs really are very short! He said, "You know, my friend Mr Hare, you are not a very nice person."

"And why," said old Mr Hare, "am I not a nice person?"

"Well," he said, "every time we meet you're always talking about my legs. I can't help it that I've got short legs, because I was born like this."

Mr Hare said, "Wouldn't you like to have long legs like me?

The Hedgehog's Race

You know I've got beautiful legs.
I can run faster than anyone!
Dogs can't even catch me.
Wouldn't it be nice if your legs
were like mine and you could run
fast as the wind across the fields?"
And old Mr Hedgehog said,
"Well, of course it would be nice
to have long legs
like you. But you
see, Mr Hare,
you don't
need long
legs to
run fast,
you
know."

"You don't need long legs to run fast?" said old Mr Hare. "Nonsense! How in the world could you run fast with those short little legs you've got? No way could you run out of the way of a dog or a fox, like me. As for me, I can run swifter than the wind!"

"Well," said old Mr Hedgehog, "you see, my friend, I'll tell you what I'll do with you. I'll make a bargain with you. I'll challenge you to a race!"

And old Mr Hare cocked up his ears and said, "Am I hearing right? You mean you're challenging me to a race?"

"Of course!" said old Mr Hedgehog. "Are you getting deaf in your old age? I said a race!"

Old Mr Hare said, "You mean you want to race me?"

"Of course," said old Mr Hedgehog, "I want to race you! I want to prove to you for once and for all that even though I've got short legs, I can run faster than you."

"Never!" said old Mr Hare. "No way could you run faster than me."

"Well," said old Mr Hedgehog, "would you like to prove it?"

"Of course," said old Mr Hare, rubbing his paws in glee. "This is going to be fun! I'd love to prove it!"

"Well," said old Mr Hedgehog, "tomorrow morning I will meet you here at this gate and I will race you to the foot of the five-acre field.

And I'll race you back again. And
I will beat you. Will you promise
me one thing?"

"Anything," said old Mr Hare,
"I'll promise you!"

"That you'll never call me Short
Legs again as long as you live!"

Old Mr Hare said, "Look, if you
want to race me, I'll race you. And
then I'll beat you like you've
never been beat in all your life.
And I'll go so fast you will never
even see me pass you by. And after
I beat you I will go on calling
you Short Legs all the days of
your life!"

"Well," said old Mr Hedgehog,

"we'll just have to wait and see."

"Done!" said old Mr Hare.
"Tomorrow morning at daybreak
I'm going to teach you a lesson
you will never forget!"

"Well," said old Mr Hedgehog,
"we'll just have to wait and see.
But remember now, Mr Hare, I'll
be here."

"Oh," said old Mr Hare, "I'll
be here!"

And like that
off went Mr Hare
for his breakfast
in the farmer's
turnip field.
But what

do you think old Mr Hedgehog did? He toddled away back to his little nest where his old wife lived, old Mrs Hedgehog! And he said, "My dear, would you do something for me?"

Of course, old Mrs Hedgehog, she loved her old husband Mr Hedgehog very much. She said, "Of course, husband, I'll do anything for you!"

He said, "You see, my dear, I've challenged Mr Hare to a race."

She said, "Husband, have you gone out of your mind? Have you gone crazy?"

"No, my dear, I've not gone crazy.

But," he said, "if you will agree to help me, I will teach old Mr Hare a lesson he will never forget."

She said, "What do you want me to do, husband?"

"Well," he said, "it's so simple! You know, old Mr Hare thinks he's very clever. But he's not as clever as he thinks he is. Because,

like everyone else, he doesn't
know you from me." (Neither do
I! If you met two hedgehogs, you
wouldn't know a Mr from a Mrs,
would you?)

"Well," she said, "husband, what
do you want me to do?"

He said, "My dear, all I want
you to do is . . . I want you to
wait till daybreak. I will wait up at
the top of the gate till Mr Hare
comes down from the hillside,
from his bush. And I will
challenge him to a race. But I'm
not going to run any, and neither
are you! I want you to wait at the
foot of the field. And when old

Mr Hare comes down to the foot of the field all you have to do is just stand up and say, 'I'm here before you!' And I will wait up at the top of the gate and I won't move. Silly old Mr Hare will never know you from me!" So the plan was made.

That night, after giving her old husband Mr Hedgehog a little cuddle, off she went. And she wandered away down to the foot of the field. There she

waited. It was summertime, the nights were not very long. And of course old Mr Hare was very bright in the morning. He liked to be up early, half past four when the sun came up! So old Mr Hedgehog, he crawled away to the gate and there he waited. He never looked for a worm, he never looked for a snail. He waited for Mr Hare!

But soon as the sun began to rise, down came old Mr Hare, so proud of himself. He was going to show old Mr Hedgehog this morning how to run – like he'd never run before in all his life.

And then he was going to go on
calling him Short Legs every time
they met. See? And many other
things forbyes. Slow Coach and
things like that!
So when Mr Hare came to the
gate, there sat old Mr Hedgehog.

He said, "Good morning, Short
Legs, are you ready?"

Of course, Mr Hedgehog, who
was very sensitive about his short
legs, said, "You promised you
wouldn't call me Short Legs any
more!"

He said, "Of course, I promised
you – but after the race! You've
not beat me yet. And you don't

have one single chance in this world. I'm going to beat you, and this morning because I feel so frisky I'm going to show you what it's like to run! After I beat you I'm going to go on calling you Short Legs all your life and many other things forbyes!"

Well, said old Mr Hedgehog, thinking to himself, *she'll be at the bottom of the field by this time.* He was happy. He said, "OK, Mr Hare, are you ready?"

And Mr Hare said, "As ready as I'll ever be!" He rubbed his paws together and said, "One, two, three – off we go!"

And old Mr Hare, off he flew down that field faster than he'd ever run. Old Mr Hedgehog sat there and watched him running like he'd never run before in his life. But he was in for a big surprise. When he came to the foot of the field, there in front of him was old Mrs Hedgehog.

She said, "I'm here before you!"

And quick as a light old Mr Hare turned and he ran back up the field as fast as he could. But on the way up he ran faster! When he came to the top of the field, there was old Mr Hedgehog.

And old Mr Hedgehog said, "I'm here before you!"

Quick as a light old Mr Hare he turned again and down that field he ran, faster than he ever ran before! But when he came to the foot of the field there was old Mrs Hedgehog!

She said, "I'm here before you!" And of course poor old Mr Hare, not knowing Mrs Hedgehog from Mr Hedgehog, he turned again! Up the field he flew as fast as he could run.

But then old Mr Hedgehog said, "I'm still here before you!"

So up and down and up and

down ran old Mr Hare, till at last
he was completely exhausted.
He could not run another step. He
came up to the top of the field
and he was lying there, his tongue
hanging out. And he was panting.

He said, "Tell me, Mr Hedgehog,
tell me, please! How
in the world did
you ever do it?
you ever do it?
You ran so fast
I never even
saw you pass
me by!"

"Of course," said old Mr Hedgehog, "I told you! You wouldn't believe me that you don't need long legs to run fast, you know!"

"Well," said old Mr Hare, "you really beat me there and I'm still not sure how you did it, but I promise you, my friend, I will never call you Short Legs again as long as I live!"

And that's why today, if you're up in the gorse hills, in the woods, you will find hedgehogs and hares asleep in the same bush – because they are very good friends! And as for old Mr Hare, he never called Mr Hedgehog Short Legs again. But of course you and I know that he beat him by a trick, didn't he? But we ain't going to tell Mr Hare, are we?

How the Lemur Got Her Tail

Mary Hoffman

Long, long ago, before there was
you, before there was me, before
there were any other people in the
world, Lemur lived in Africa. She
was grey all over then, with a
long, bushy grey tail which she
held high above her back like a
flag. The other animals could
always see her coming as she
walked across the forest floor.

"Good morning, Lemur," called Chameleon, flicking out his long, sticky tongue. "Where are you off to this hot, sunny morning?"

"I'm going across the water," said Lemur, "where the Baobab trees are shady and the sweet figs grow. Why don't you come too?

So the Chameleon followed after. He was slower than Lemur, but he didn't get lost because he could always see her bushy tail. Up in the air flew Red

Kingfisher. "Good morning, Lemur," he sang. "Where are you and Chameleon off to this hot, sunny morning?"

"We're going across the water," said Lemur, "where the rivers are cool and the flowers shine bright in the dark green forest. Why don't you come too?"

So the Red Kingfisher went with them. He could fly much faster than they could walk, but he didn't lose them because he could always see Lemur's bushy tail waving above the grass.

Green Boa Snake was
slithering across the forest floor.
"Good morning, Lemur,"
she hissed. "Where are you
and Chameleon and Red
Kingfisher off to this hot and
sunny morning?"

"We're going across the water,"
said Lemur, "where the rain is
warm and the nights are cool.
Why don't you come too?"

So the Green Boa Snake joined
them. She could move quickly,
even though she had no legs. And
if she lost them, she could slink
up a tree and look out for Lemur's
bushy tail.

As they passed a tree branch,
Tiny Golden Frog croaked, "Good
morning, Lemur. Where are you
going with Chameleon, Red
Kingfisher and Green Boa Snake
this hot, sunny morning?"

"We're going across the water,"
said Lemur, "where the mountains
are red and the Great Bamboo
grows up to the sky. Why
don't you come too?"

So the Tiny Gold
Frog joined them,
leaping from tree to
tree with his long,
strong back legs and looking out for
the grey flag that was Lemur's tail.

Pansy Butterfly darted back and forth in the warm morning air, fluttering her gorgeous blue wings.

"Good morning, Lemur," she chirped. "Where are you going with Chameleon, Red Kingfisher, Green Boa Snake and Tiny Golden Frog this hot, sunny morning?"

"We're going across the water," said Lemur, "where the bees make honey from orchids and the wild ginger grows. Why don't you come too?"

So Pansy Butterfly flitted along above the other animals, keeping an eye on Lemur's tail.

Suddenly, all the animals noticed

that Lemur had stopped. She had
come to the edge of the water.
The others stopped too and
looked at the land across the water
that was so full of good things.

"It's all very well for Red
Kingfisher and Pansy Butterfly,"
said Chameleon doubtfully, "but
how are the rest of us going to
get across? The water looks very
wide and deep to me."

"It is," said Lemur, "but look again. There are little islands and ridges under the water all the way across.

You'll be there in a leap, skip and jump."

And to show that she was right, she leapt into the water, waving her bushy grey tail to keep her balance as she hopscotched her way across to the other side. All the others followed one by one. It was easiest for Tiny Golden Frog and hardest for Green Boa Snake, but they all got to the other side in the end.

The warm sun soon dried them out and Lemur led the way to her favourite places. They all found good things to eat – berries and nuts and nectar. It was midday by then and everyone was feeling full and hot and sleepy.

Lemur stretched out in the shade of a Baobab tree. She was so full of figs that she forgot to keep her tail out of the hot sun. She stayed awake just long enough to curl her paws round her eyes to keep out the glare. Then she fell into a deep sleep.

When everyone woke up, it was late and the long shadows of evening were falling through the green forest.

"We must go back," croaked Tiny Golden Frog. "Where's Lemur? She must show us the way."

"There she is," said Pansy Butterfly. "She's still asleep. I'll go down and wake her up."

And the beautiful blue butterfly
flew down and perched on
Lemur's nose. So tickly were her
little feet that Lemur woke up
with a sneeze. Pansy Butterfly
flew away in alarm.

"What's happened to your face, Lemur?" she shrieked, "and oh, what is the matter with your tail?"

All the animals crowded round to see what had happened to Lemur in her sleep. The fierce sun had broken through the trees and bleached her face white. Round her eyes, where she had shaded them with her paws, there were two big, black circles. And her long bushy tail, which had been stretched out on the forest floor, was now striped black and white — black where the shade of the branches had protected some bits from the sun, white where the

sun's powerful midday rays had
shone down and bleached it.

Lemur led them all down to the
water so that she could look at
her reflection. She
turned this way and
that and waved her
tail around.

"It's not bad, you know, Lemur," hissed Green Boa Snake. "We'll be able to see where you are even better now."

"Yes," said Red Kingfisher. "And now you should lead the others back over the water."

But something else had happened while the animals were asleep. The water was deeper and wider and all the little underwater islands and ridges had disappeared. The animals couldn't go back. Red Kingfisher and Pansy Butterfly could have flown over the water, but they decided to stay with their friends.

They are all living there still.
After all, the great island across the
water from Africa was full of good
things. Its name is Madagascar.
And Ring-tailed Lemur still runs
across the forest floor there,
holding up her tail like a flag, for
all her friends and family to see.

Clever Rabbit and King Lion

Amoafi Kwapong

Once upon a time, and a very good time it was, there lived in the rainforest of Ghana many animals and Lion was their king.

King Lion lived in the best cave on one side of the forest while the rest of the animals shared the other side. The other animals were not amused but they had no choice than to remain where they were.

Clever Rabbit was a very close friend of Madam Hare. Clever Rabbit was very quick at solving problems and riddles which earned her the title of "Clever". Madam Hare was known in the whole wide forest as a kind-hearted lady. With her long ears, Madam Hare could hear a long way away.

One day, Madam Hare overheard King Lion talking to his wife. He was boasting about a plan of his to eat up Clever Rabbit. He had already eaten most of the little animals in the forest.

"Today," he said, "it's Clever Rabbit's turn."

Madam Hare was very upset. She hurried to tell Clever Rabbit what she had heard. At first Clever Rabbit was very upset too. She thought to herself, *I mind my own business and I don't deserve this.* Madam Hare tried to console her, but Clever Rabbit said, "Action is what I need."

Clever Rabbit had a quick think and she came up with an idea.

"I'll go to King Lion's cave and offer myself to him. I bet he'll be so confused he won't eat me just yet."

"Very good," replied Madam Hare.

Clever Rabbit set out for King Lion's cave.

Meanwhile, King Lion was on his way to Clever Rabbit's burrow. Halfway down the path, King Lion and Clever Rabbit met face to face. King Lion's eyes were red and he looked fierce. Clever Rabbit put on a brave face and a smile. She greeted King Lion, "Good morning, Your Majesty. I heard you were going to eat me up for dinner today. So I wanted to make it easier for you by offering myself to you."

149

"Don't be cheeky, you little rascal," answered King Lion.

Clever Rabbit continued, "I didn't mean to be cheeky, Your Majesty, but on second thoughts I don't think you'll enjoy eating me just yet. Give me three weeks to fatten up for you. You see, I'm all bones."

"Very well," retorted King Lion. "I can wait three weeks."

150

So off went Clever Rabbit to her burrow, stopping on the way to tell Madam Hare the good news. "Hooray! Hooray!" cried the two friends.

A week passed but Clever Rabbit looked the same. A second week passed and still Clever Rabbit had not added an ounce of flesh to her skinny body.

After two weeks King Lion began to count the seconds, the minutes, the hours. Day one came and went. Then it was day two, day three, day four, day five, day six and day seven!

"Three weeks are up! I'm going

to feast on rabbit today!" gloated King Lion.

Clever Rabbit dressed in her prettiest clothes with bows in her hair. On her way to King Lion's cave she stopped to chat with Madam Hare. Madam Hare wished Clever Rabbit the best of luck saying, "I trust that you'll come back again."

"Thank you," said Clever Rabbit, "I certainly need a lot of luck today." And off she went.

When she arrived at King Lion's cave, King Lion was working up his appetite. He was just about to pounce on Clever Rabbit when she said, "Oh, Your Majesty, you should hear this! There's a bigger lion not too far away from here who's been competing with you.

He's eating all the little animals there and I hear he's eaten more than you have."

"Is that so?" said King Lion. "Show me the way to this arrogant lion and I'll soon sort him out."

Clever Rabbit led the way. She was so overjoyed at not being gobbled up by King Lion that she began to sing, dance and skip along the path. King Lion was not amused. He roared at Clever Rabbit, "Stop singing, dancing and skipping at once!" Clever Rabbit stopped at once.

Soon they were both standing by a lake. Clever Rabbit pointed to a spot where King Lion should stand and look in the water. King Lion quickly stood on that spot and stretched to look in the water. There was another lion! Quick as a flash, King Lion

jumped into the lake to fight the other lion.

Too late, he realized that Clever Rabbit had tricked him! He struggled to get out of the water. But as you and I know, cats (even big cats) can't swim too well. King Lion drowned and Clever Rabbit was free to sing, dance and skip again. She sang and danced and skipped all the way back to Madam Hare who was waiting anxiously.

Clever Rabbit and Madam Hare sang, danced and skipped together all night long. And when the other little animals of the rainforest

heard what had happened, they
hurried to join in the celebration.

The story that you've just heard,
take it with you and share it.

Acknowledgements

'Crocodile Tears' reproduced by permission of the Agency (London) Ltd © Joyce Dunbar 1994. First published by Kingfisher Publications; 'Hot Hippos' copyright © Sally Grindley 1994; 'How the Lemur Got Her Tail' copyright © Mary Hoffman 1994; 'Hungry Hari' copyright © Dick King-Smith 1994; 'Clever Rabbit and King Lion' copyright © Amoafi Kwapong 1991; 'Slowly Does It' copyright © Robin Ravilious 1994; 'The Little Elephant's Next Best Thing' copyright © Mary Rayner 1989; The Magpie's Nest copyright © Michael Rosen 1989; 'The Hedgehog's Race' copyright © Duncan Williamson 1991; 'The Lamb Who Couldn't Sleep' copyright © John Yeoman 1991.

While every effort has been made to obtain permission, there may still be cases where we have failed to trace a copyright holder. We would like to apologize for any omissions; we are happy to correct these in future printings.